THE NEW GIRLS' PATIENT

RUTHANN JAGGE

D & T
PUBLISHING

To my husband Michael, who has put up with me for 25 years and thinks everything I write is a masterpiece.

Your love and support make it all possible and without limits.

ACKNOWLEDGMENTS

Writing is the hardest and best work I've ever done, and I couldn't do it without the support of my family, friends, and the fantastic horror community at large.

I'd like to thank Dawn Shea, Tim Shea, and the entire D&T Team for their brilliant creative opportunities and generous, kind and professional encouragement.

Thanks to Editor Patrick C. Harrison III for his many skills and dark humor. Every good story needs a patient editor to make it better.

Thank you, Don Noble, for creating the beautiful cover art representing my story. I am in awe of your talent.

I'm always thankful for the many devoted reviewers who keep authors humble and grateful.

Thank you to the readers who spend valuable time with the stories we tell. Without you, the effort would go unnoticed.

THE NEW GIRLS' PATIENT

CREES CROSSING IS UNREMARKABLE. The rural southern town is barely a dot on any map. It's a stop if you're desperate for fuel or a cold drink, but never a destination. The area has no notable citizens, remarkable architecture, or exciting history attracting visitors.

It does have a past.

Appearances matter to most folks, whether they have little or a lot. You look after and protect your family even if they are the darkest story you've ever heard.

Jamie Carver slams the door twice, making sure the broken metal lock clicks. A casualty of an attempted break-in under previous ownership. Her home is old and needs repairs. The single-wide trailer cost a thousand dollars down and a small amount payable on the third of each month. The narrow aluminum structure leans to the left on a plot of land on the outskirts of Crees Crossing, surrounded by dry fields. Years of tobacco crops stripped the land of life, and only squash and pumpkin grow there now.

She's obligated to working irregular shifts at the local hospital, but Jamie knows she's lucky to have a decent-paying job. There aren't many to choose from these days. Working at the outdated, under-staffed care facility erases her commitment to the government for the introductory nursing course she recently completed. Mercy Care is not a place people go to get better, but more of a long-term storage unit for those who don't. The once impressive, decaying brick structure built in the late 1930s houses elderly residents without financial resources or loving family interested in them.

No one expected recent funding cutbacks for public health services to hit the area so hard, but as a result, her hours are limited and inconsistent. Noon to 5 or 6pm a few days a week makes for a considerably lighter paycheck. She does errands and spends time in the garden during the morning, with good intentions of making it to a workout class at the high school gym in the evening. Jamie doesn't own a vehicle, so she rides her bike or walks in nice weather, accepting rides when necessary. A guy she knew in high school started a dial-a-ride business a few months ago, but the law arrested him for selling stolen pills to passengers, ending the operation abruptly.

Like many places, Crees Crossing has more than its share of boozers and losers. The parking lot of the Dollar Daze is full of old chicken bones, used pregnancy tests, and a cast of permanently down-on-their-luck regulars, sharing cold tallboys while staring at their free phones. The beer hits different when you celebrate another day accomplishing nothing. Rumors of hidden whiskey stills and entire families of drug-cookers living deep in the nearby woods are the topic of everyday gossip. Jamie's mom raised her to keep her distance from things and people lacking in good intentions.

Laine Carver was a petite and pretty woman who didn't do well with everyday life and preferred her garden to most people. She kept to herself. Jamie loved listening to her stories and songs while Laine baked juicy pies with fruit picked from the apple and cherry trees growing in the yard. She sold them for dessert at a local diner and kept the money in a cardboard oatmeal box. Some believed gentle Laine was simple-minded instead of kind and grounded. She was a person with her unique ways of doing things and managed to keep Jamie fed and warm without the opinions or resources of others. The money she made selling produce and dark glass bottles of herbal tinctures during the Summer wasn't much, but it was enough to get by, and they thrived together. Sometimes, young women would knock on the door late at night, needing Laine's advice, asking for special herbs to fix particular problems. A couple of years ago, Jamie found her mother's body in the garden. She appeared to be resting peacefully except for a significant purple mark radiating up one leg; a venomous snake bit her ankle. Her mother would disapprove of an organized funeral, so Jamie buried Laine herself under the fruit trees she loved while singing their favorite songs. There was no one to protest her actions.

Jamie doesn't remember her Father, Marvin Carver. He died tragically in a fire when she was very young. Marvin was a business owner by definition, repairing the occasional car or motorcycle in their driveway. He was a skilled mechanic who could build or fix anything with wheels. The official report claimed a fuel leak caused the fire, but folks say he owed more money in gambling debts than he ever made, and Marvin paid back his creditors with interest. Small town bullshit is consistent in its smallness for the most part, and Jamie learned this from a young age, keeping to herself and focusing on better things. There isn't any other close family she's aware of, so she sells off what little remains in their run-down rented home for pennies on the dollar after her mom dies, using the money to buy her place on the mean acre of well-used land.

Jamie needs to support herself and applies for a housekeeping job at the hospital, hoping there will be time for daydreams later. She's unsure of her future in Crees Crossing, and the options are limited. The pleasant, reserved young woman catches the eye of an older nurse, eager to retire, who notices she's a hard worker, intelligent and reliable, and always kind to the state-funded patients living on borrowed time. The hospital is known locally as God's Rural Waiting Room. The residents are admitted by an uncaring family or the court, with the ultimate intention of a more humane passing. The nurse suggests Jamie fill out the required paperwork and sign up online for an accredited nursing class, offering to add her personal and professional recommendations to the process.

The girl doesn't own a computer, so she stays on after her shift, eating jelly sandwiches while studying alone in a small office with management approval. She completes the required clinical work, passes her exam, and starts earning a slightly better salary at the hospital soon after.

The first few months in her position at Mercy Care are tough. Jamie is the unofficial new girl. She's assigned the dirty work others neglect but doesn't miss a shift, does her job well, and gains respect as a valued employee. The run-down facility relies on her. Patient care is minimal but consistent, and Jamie's confident she's chosen a solid career path to build on, hoping for more education and experience. She makes a couple of friends at work, sharing stories and making weekend plans with them at lunch. They discuss their love lives over tuna salad, or rather the lack of, due to only a few young men worth dating in the entire county.

Lila Walker, the daughter of a sharecropper, is no stranger to working hard and has a few years of professional nursing experience under her belt. Calista Crees is the granddaughter of the man who had founded Crees Crossing, and she's the only "better off" person Jamie and Lila know. She's a new addition to the hospital, filling a recently created patient advocate position designated by the state. The three young women cover the random hours not claimed by three more experienced nurses on staff. Crees family donations built the hospital years ago, and Calista's job is an easy one compared to the others.

As Jamie walks down the narrow hallway, Lila calls to her from a patient's room. She's holding a glass of water steady for a small bald man sipping cautiously through a straw. Lila's compassion is exceptional, and she treats the residents as if they are as well.

"Hey there, you, let's try and make the new Dance A Lot class over at the high school gym. It starts at six. I've already wrangled the other heifer, and after all the snacks she's been munching working grave-yard, she sure needs it."

Jamie laughs, nodding her agreement and noticing grey streaks on the walls from a recent scrubbing. Everything at Mercy is shabby and well-used but clean for the most part.

Cally is short and plain, with unstylish chunky frosted brown hair, but has all the best-looking dirty boys talking to her when the three friends stop by the least pathetic local watering hole Saturday nights for a few light beers and a game of pool. The girl is flashy and bold, with her ample assets compensating for her lack of good looks. She always has the most and loudest fun in any social setting. She doesn't need to worry about money or plans; her wealthy family provides substantial resources and funds to their offspring through long-established trust funds.

Lila couldn't care less about attracting anyone. She's a stunning natural beauty who also has a mysterious long-term boyfriend she claims to love, off fighting somewhere in the desert. The gorgeous young woman is content to get a letter or a call from her soldier every couple of months. Lila's a trusted friend; the girls grew up together on the sad side of town. Cally is a new acquaintance, eager for acceptance. Jamie gets her share of whiskey-soaked offers and heavy-handed gropes on the dance floor. Still, she's focused on learning to be the best caregiver possible, hoping to enjoy life more on her terms eventually, once she figures them out, preferably somewhere else. She thinks about moving often but knows she needs to save money for a vehicle and earn more experience for a better job in a bigger hospital.

The care facility's routine is more challenging today; one of the regular nurses is out sick with a cold, so they're short-staffed. The typically calm residents are restless because even simple tasks are taking longer, and a regular daily routine is essential to them. Jamie hits the floor running the minute she signs into her shift. It's almost 5pm when she notices the door to one of her favorite patient's rooms at the end of the dingy-green painted corridor is closed for longer than usual. She only knows the occupant of the room as Miz Elizabeth. The frail older woman has never spoken while Jamie's worked at Mercy. She spends most of her day writing and shares her few needs with staff on neatly folded notes. Jamie opens the door. The bed is empty, linens are gone, and the room smells recently cleaned. The air has the stink of cheap lavender-scented antiseptic. The sticky sweetness clings to her uniform and won't wash off in the shower. The scent means death to Jamie. A housekeeper dressed in loose blue scrubs peeks out from the tiny white tiled bathroom with a sponge in her hand.

"She went without warning, and we found her right before you signed in. I think she left something for you, so check up front when you sign out."

Jamie swallows back the lump in her throat, reminding herself this happens frequently. There's more death than life at Mercy.

She enjoyed reading to the sweet woman with the watery blue eyes when it wasn't busy. Miz Elizabeth never had any visitors, so she'd bring her a few wildflowers in a jelly jar and make sure she got a small piece of cake if there was a party in the lunchroom. She helped her wash and change her thin white cotton nightgown several times a day. A neat row of the long, floaty garments hung in her closet. She owned no other clothing. Jamie gently brushed her soft, remarkably long silver hair, and it curled over her shoulders in thick waves. Miz Elizabeth always managed a small smile when she handed her a compact mirror to admire the results. The silent woman was a memorable patient, and Jamie already misses her. She promises the room she'll light a candle and say a prayer for her on the rare days she remembers to pray. For the residents of Mercy, death is inevitable. Her shift is almost over, and for a while, life goes on.

"Lila says we're going to the workout class at the high school tonight. My car's parked outback. I'll wait for y'all to quit playing around and get shit done." Cally clicks the lock on the door to her private office, formerly a mop closet, smacking Jamie's butt as she passes by.

"Sounds good. Maybe we can grab a salad after if you don't have a better offer." Jamie smacks her back, giggling. Cally is the only one who owns a reliable vehicle, and she hates being alone almost as much as she hates her family, so they tend to spend a few evenings together.

The New Girl grabs her nylon gym bag from the locker and heads to the front desk. Almost no one refers to her as Jamie. The bored receptionist sitting at the table in the admitting area snaps her gum loudly and wears too much eyeliner. She glances over the top of her magazine.

"She left this for you. It's ugly, but I'm supposed to make sure you get it, so here." She's holding out what looks like an old pillow-case with worn rope handles. The initials "E C" are stitched in heavy black thread on one side. Jamie nods her thanks and reaches into the threadbare cotton feed sack. It contains a folded note written on a scrap of paper and a worn black and white school composition notebook with "My Recipes" written in a shaky hand on the front cover.

"Thanks." Jamie quickly flips through what appears to be a collec-tion of handwritten recipes. There are explanations of how to prepare and preserve food. Lines of hard-to-read numbers and strange little drawings are scratched randomly on the pages in black ink. She unfolds the note.

"Grateful for your kindness, E.C."

Pushing everything back into the sack, she shoves it into her gym bag and heads down the only hallway leading to the back parking lot. She's not much of a cook but plans to look at the book again later; out of respect to her favorite patient, maybe she'll pick up a few ideas and cook herself a healthy meal for a change.

Summer is almost over and it's getting dark earlier. Jamie feels the snappy night breeze kicking up as she pushes in the locking bar securing the exit and opens the heavily scratched metal door. *E T.* The blinking red *EXIT* sign needs new lightbulbs. Just about everything at the hospital needs fixing.

Cally's car is running but still parked with the door wide open. Jamie squints to focus with the fading daylight, and she sees Lila lying on the ground holding her leg in a dark puddle of what looks like blood. Her phone lies in pieces on the cracked blacktop out of her reach with its pink glitter cover smashed.

Jamie makes out the shapes of two men: one is squatty and wears rumpled denim mechanic's overalls; the other man is tall and muscular with a thick dark beard and a camouflage ball cap. He has a large hunting knife in his hand. They're folding Cally, who isn't moving, roughly into the back seat of her car.

Janie chokes on a scream, trying to kick the door open again, intending to find help, but the approaching darkness triggers the solar timer on the lock. It refuses to open. She struggles to keep her balance, hitting the light on her phone repeatedly. She's pounding madly on the insulated door, screaming, when the bearded one grabs her by the hair, clamping a huge hand smelling of cigarettes over her mouth. The big man yanks her off her feet, dragging her toward the car. Her phone flies from her hand as she violently swings her gym bag at his knees. But she misses. He laughs and pulls harder at her hair, flinging the bag into the car. He bangs her head hard on the door frame, kicking her inside with his laced boot.

"You won't be able to move anymore if you don't knock off your shit, and you're dead if you scream again!" He grabs at her breasts, snarling.

He smells like cat pee. Jamie tries to breathe, gulping in the air, fighting off full-on hysteria. She watches them throw Lila, screeching like an owl and making terrible gurgling sounds, into the trunk. The men hoot and holler as it slams shut, clapping each other on the shoulder. There's no one coming to help.

Cally looks to be in shock or near death. Jamie can't tell because her head slumps ungracefully against the window on the opposite side of the backseat. Blood is streaming down her face, and she senses her friend is badly hurt. She wants to shake her awake, but Jamie is fighting to breathe and stay conscious as fear rips through her mind. She knows her life depends on staying calm even though her mind is racing incoherently.

She scrambles for the handle of the door as the two men climb in, but the squatty one swings back at her quickly, hitting her face hard with Cally's phone gripped in his hand.

"Fuckin' door is already locked, Bitch. Do we look dumb?" His teeth are stained brown, and his eyes are glossy. Jamie says nothing and puts her head down. The punch hurt, but they don't deserve her tears. Her bag is in a heap on the floor. She can't remember if there's anything helpful in it, and she's too scared to look inside. She forces herself to sit still and ride along, shaking silently as the two men in front light up an awful smelling pipe

They crack open cans of cheap beer, loudly discussing *who* the real king of country music is while arguing over radio stations, and the squatty one scrolls through the photos on Cally's phone for entertainment. The Beard, as Jamie thinks of him, seems to be the brains of the abduction.

"Damn, this ripe cow is nasty. Check it out. Bitch is sexting Tommy Alford, and you know the dude is married tight. His old lady will cut his balls off if she finds out. I might blackmail her ass if she still has one when we finish with her, and maybe his too." Squatty holds the phone up close to Beard's face, and he glances over at the screen.

"Got some miles on her. Not too bad, though. I might have a go at that ass with a few of my special homemade toys for shits and grins. I like it when they scream bloody murder." They pass the pipe between them, sucking on it hard. The squatty one laughs with an evil snorting sound, pointing at the screen.

Their disgusting comments make Jamie cringe and shake, wanting to cover her ears or kill them, and she's glad when Squatty decides to toss it out the window of the moving vehicle. Blackmail would require too much effort on his part.

"Enough of this shit." There are no lights on the dark, bumpy gravel road. Cally's compact car lurches along as Jamie tries hard to make out a landmark or get her bearings. But she has no idea where they are, and even the stars seem too far away to care. Cally is still not responding. Jamie wonders if her worst nightmare is better than the current situation. She wants to scream until she passes out and wakes up home safe in her bed.

The car finally stops in front of an old house with a yard full of weeds, surrounded by a circle of tall trees. She hears the leaves rustling on the limbs, and a thought passes through her mind.

I might not be here for Autumn Fest this year.

The two-storied house is decrepit and in miserable condition but stood impressive at one time. It has layers of chipped white paint on the ornately carved railings, and the elegantly designed curved porch is hanging half off. The slate-tiled roof sags dangerously, threatening to collapse, and most of the wavy glass in the vintage windows is cracked or shattered.

Everyone Jamie knows lives in trailers like herself or small wood-framed shacks considered shabby by anyone's standards. For a split second, she feels sorry for the crumbling mansion. It deserves a better end than simply falling to dust.

Stinking of alcohol and whatever garbage they smoked to get a buzz, the men get out of the car. The Beard opens the back door pulling Jamie out by her leg as he points his big knife with the jagged blade at her face.

"Girl, you aren't ugly, but I like my women nasty, so don't make me mad, or I'll slice your nose clean off!" As her body slams to the ground, she grabs for her gym bag clutching at the nylon straps. He pulls her roughly along in the dirt by one ankle, and Jamie feels small sharp stones cutting into her back. Her arm bangs against something hard, and the pain shoots through her like an arrow, but she forces herself to go limp. When he lets go of her leg, the girl manages to roll, hiding the bag under her. He bends down, shaking the knife in her face again. She whimpers, pulling away.

"Please. No. I'll do anything you want. Just don't hurt me." He licks her cheek, and Jamie swallows down her disgust. Giving in might be her best chance at staying alive.

"I know you will. I just ain't in the mood yet." He backhands Jamie's cheek.

The Beard spins around, smacking the knife hard against a padlock that holds a pair of heavy cracked wooden cellar doors at the rear of the house closed. It flies off, and he kicks one rusty-hinged door open to the side. The horrible stench of deep rot seeping into the air is worse than anything Jamie can imagine, and she gags back her fear, coughing as he yanks her up by her arms until she's almost standing. He slowly licks her cheek again, nuzzling her hair and breathing her in. She feels him grow hard against her leg, and she decides to do whatever is necessary to survive. She reaches down with both hands, grabbing for him, but instead, he shoves her down the steps. She lands in a heap on the damp concrete floor with her ankle twisted under her, still clinging to her gym bag. Waves of pain blind her.

Squatty is dragging Cally from the car. She's awake and screaming, hurling insults and swearing her head off. She's kicking at him, flailing her arms in circles like a windmill, trying to land a punch. Her face and shoulders drip with blood, and her hair appears soaked with it. She looks like she's wearing a red cartoon wig. The Beard comes at her from behind, jerking her arms back. Cally screams to wake the dead. He's holding his knife to her throat, clawing at her crotch to hold her up. Squatty, hanging over himself from exertion, catches his breath.

"TJ, you piece of shit, you half-wit moron!" Cally screams. "What you're doing is bullshit. I told you I would get it. You fuckin' fat slob! Let go of me, or I'll kill you both, you shit-bag ass-wipe!"

The Beard snickering at her warnings, steps around like a boxer and punches Cally in the stomach hard. She gasps for air, thrashing wildly as they both grab an arm, hurling her down the steps. She keeps screaming and threatening as she hits every hard surface on the way down.

"This is *not* the plan, you fuckers! You're such assholes. You've done it now!"

Cally has a large open gash on the back of her head, in need of many stitches, and her bloodied face scares Jamie even more, if that's possible. Her teeth are red, coated with blood, but she keeps screaming hysterically as the men bang the doors above shut. The young woman tries scrambling up the steps like a crab on all fours, but her limbs don't respond to her injured brain. She falls back onto the concrete, banging her head yet again. Cally lies there sobbing, moaning in agony. Jamie crawls to her friend, breathing raggedly through the stench, but when she puts her hand on Cally's arm, anxious to help with her wounds, she slaps it away.

"Don't you touch me? You have no idea how bad this is!" They both curl into fetal positions on the moldy floor. Cally lies motionless, Jamie considers passing out. She fights the raging pain in her ankle and slowly drags herself to a corner, struggling to focus. Besides the awful smell of rotting cabbage and roadkill, it's cold and damp in the cellar. It's filthy and dark, and the only light filters in through a few cracks. There's a large wooden table, some boxes, a few old barrels, and some rows of dusty glass mason jars filled with spoiled goods lining metal utility shelves leaned against the cement walls. It appears to be a root cellar, dug out deep under the house, intended for storage.

The doors above squeal open again, and Lila's body bumps down the steps. Their beautiful friend's flesh oozes with fresh blood, and her face is purple with bruises. Her long dark hair, usually worn in a plump, perfect bun high on the top of her head, is ripped out in spots, and her pale scalp shows through. The remaining strands of hair stick together in bloody clumps like spikes. What remains of clothing is tattered and hanging off. Her beautiful young body is mangled beyond repair. Jamie tries to cover her friend with the few scraps she still wears as tears stream down her face.

The Beard waited in the low shrubs for Lila, the first of the trio leaving the hospital. He sliced cleanly through her Achilles' tendons with one swipe of his blade, causing her to collapse helplessly in horrible pain and bleeding badly. As they stuffed her into the trunk, he repeatedly poked at the girl with his knife, trying to shut her up, but he nicked her carotid artery in the process. When they pop the trunk open at the house, eager to scare her even more, Lila is already gone, dying alone, afraid, and smothering in her blood.

Her fatal condition doesn't stop the two men from having a good time; she's too pretty to ignore. It doesn't bother them she can't kiss back. Rough sex without slapping and biting is just as much fun as long as she's still a little warm inside. Jamie screams until she's dizzy, holding the body of her sweet friend as Cally, now awake and fixating on the stairs, refuses to look at what's left of Lila.

"How could they do this to you?" Jamie holds Lila's body in her arms. "I'm so sorry. I'm so sorry I couldn't save you." Lila's corpse plops heavily to the floor with Jamie still holding her hand, she can't stop crying over her, but she curses the pair, swearing revenge, even if she dies trying.

"I told you, this is bad news!" Cally spits the words at Jamie through the blood on her face, drooling long red strings. "Do you honestly believe I'm your friend, you stupid cow? Do you think I give a rat's ass about you? I wouldn't piss on you if you were on fire. My family owned this town before your hick-ass was even born!"

Jamie flinches at the hatred in her voice. Cally's words echo in her ears, and her head is pounding.

"You don't know shit, bitch, but you sure will before this is over, you haven't seen anything yet!" Cally turns away, hugging her knees tight to her chest. "They're going to kill us in this stinking hole, and it's probably my fault. I feel sick. I don't want to die, but trust me, we *are* going to die in here." She rubs at her head, smearing her bloody hands on her pink scrubs, trying to pinch and seal the gaping wound with her fingers. The blood flows out faster. Giving up, she collapses.

There's loud music and howls of laughter coming from above. Something smells acrid and sour, and it's making Jamie nauseous. She hears bugs and probably rats in the walls doing their awful dance. Crawling weakly back to the corner where her gym bag lies in the shadows, she fights with the zipper, trying to open it in case there's something she can use to defend herself or eat or anything useful at all.

She rifles through the cheap nylon bag, finding a couple of smushed protein bars and some loose change. The sack Miz Elizabeth left for her flops open, and the black and white notebook falls out. She shoves it away and keeps digging, but there's not much in there.

"Where the fuck did you get this?" Cally leans over on one side, slipping in her blood on the grimy floor, grabbing for the notebook. She flips the corners of the pages, trying to make out the contents in the dim light of the cellar.

" I SAID where in the FUCKING HELL did you get this, you BITCH?" She screams at Jamie again, smacking her hard on the shoulder with the notebook. Jamie retreats several feet. Her friend is furious, with blood still pouring down her cheek. The nasty head wound looks angrier now.

"My patient left it for me. She died earlier today, and I picked it up in reception when I signed out. It's just a bunch of old recipes, so why the hell do you care? You live on fast food." Jamie screamed back, grabbing for the notebook. It's hers and means a lot to her, unlike Cally, who now means nothing.

"Do you even KNOW who your precious Miz Elizabeth, Miz E.C. even WAS? Do you? Of course, you don't, you ignorant little trailer trash piece of shit!" She yanks the notebook back hard.

Jamie glares daggers at the bleeding girl, wanting to slap her messy face and shut her up.

"She was my GRANDMOTHER, and she lived in this hell hole!" Cally is breathing hard. Her eyes are thin dark slits trying to read the writing on the worn pages. "I know what I need is written down in here somewhere. It has to be. If I can figure this out, those boys won't kill me. You are dead meat, and I don't give a shit about you, but I can save my ass."

Jamie's thoughts are spinning out of control. None of this, not one single minute since stepping out the back door of Mercy, makes any sense. She tries to recall a thought, a memory, anything unusual during the day. She can only logically determine several hours have passed. Nothing else sticks out in her mind.

"Cally. For the love of everything good, please, tell me what's happening? There must be a way out of this, and I don't hate you. I just want to go home!" Hot tears stream as she realizes how pathetic she sounds. She's begging this raving maniac she thought was her friend for permission to stay alive; but if it works, she's willing to do it. "Dammit, please. If we stick together, we can fix this. The three of us go through lots of crazy stuff together, remember? Holy hell, I wish Lila could still talk, because you listen to her, and you look up to her because she's pretty and smart. All the boys hang at our table when we're out because they're hoping she'll notice them, not you. You take advantage and use her to snag attention and get laid. You might not owe me, but you sure do owe her, even if she's dead. So, tell me HOW we can fix this?" Jamie chokes up, trying to finish the sentence, feeling defeated.

Cally raises her head. She's tracing the letters on the cover of the black and white notebook. Her fingers are cracking, flaking with dried blood. Twisting her swollen lips, she blows out hard. Her breath turns grey in the chilly cellar. Then she leans back against a wooden barrel, the pain and loss of blood affect her ability to speak. She's scared. Maybe if she comes clean with Jamie, she won't die like a dog.

"My grandmother, Elizabeth, was fifteen when her father sold her to Lonnie Crees for twenty dollars, a couple of jugs of shine, and forty-five leaves of tobacco. Her mother died giving birth, and he hated the girl. She was too small to be much good around the place. She cost him money. He blamed her for everything wrong in his life. Elizabeth kept to herself and out of his way, or there was hell to pay.

"Lonnie was an ambitious young man, the son of a prominent tobacco farmer. He wasn't much to look at, so women avoided his advances. The arrogant male was, however, in the market for a wife. Lonnie decided Elizabeth would be easy prey; her father didn't want her, and she had no foreseeable future. She didn't have a family to contend with, and she'd be an asset to him for minimal effort or expense. He planned on running a tight ship just like his daddy did. She'd work damn hard making him happy or else. Crees men enjoyed disciplining their women, and he looked forward to it. The young girl's sparkly blue eyes and nice figure were a bonus. He also planned on getting a couple of heirs out of her to help on the farm. He might get rid of her after and find another if he felt like something different. She was a good deal for now. There was no proper wedding, only a handshake agreement between the two men and a shared mason jar of moonshine. Elizabeth packed her few simple belongings and left with Lonnie, honoring their agreement, although his appearance was unpleasant, and he repulsed her. Her father ended his obligation to the girl and didn't so much as wave goodbye. Lonnie brought her to this house, one of the best in the county, but her life changed forever once she entered.

"The teen-bride learned monsters are real on her wedding night and almost every night after for years.

"Lonnie told people she was sickly; my grandmother rarely left the house because of her constant bruises and injuries. He allowed her only the barest of necessities, and while the Crees home and property looked impressive, the insides were sparse and cheaply furnished. Lonnie didn't allow any luxuries, frivolous decorations, or visitors. No one doubted the son of an upstanding member of the community, and assumed Elizabeth lived comfortably.

"Elizabeth gave Lonnie his two sons, bringing them into the world alone in a small bed. The younger one was born crippled because of beatings she suffered while carrying him, and Lonnie was disgusted by the infant, refusing to acknowledge him. Elizabeth held his tiny-mangled body, wrapped in her nightgown, and named him Jessie. She fell asleep with him by her side, exhausted by her unthinkable ordeal.

"The following day, Lonnie and the baby were gone. A couple of days later, when her husband returned alone, Elizabeth begged Lonnie to tell her if their boy was still alive

"'I sold that freak to the sideshow. If you even mention his name, whatever it was, you won't be able to repeat it when I finish with you.' He took off his belt, intending to drive his point home. After that day, Elizabeth fell into a dark hole, barely able to complete basic tasks. Emotionless, she suffered his abuse in silence. She wasn't entirely alone, though, and waited for her opportunity.

"Their older son, my father David, looked and acted exactly like his father, and she was afraid for him and of him. Elizabeth was locked in tight to herself, struggling to continue living and unable to show him affection.

"Lonnie sent my father away to be schooled by clergy when he was young, mainly to deprive Elizabeth of any joy in raising him but also to ensure he'd continue to appear respectable. A caring husband and father. The boy rarely saw his mother in the years that followed. Lonnie traveled to him, and they shared a paternal bond without his son returning home. He told my father she was unwell and needed to be locked away, so she didn't harm herself or others."

"Oh, how awful," Jamie says. "I didn't know anything about Miz Elizabeth." She wishes for one more day with her kind patient. Cally unwraps a crushed protein bar lying on the floor and tries to gulp down a mouthful, coughing on the taste of blood in her mouth.

"When things all went to shit during the '30s and the dirt dried up, Lonnie needed to figure out another way to make money because the family tobacco fields soured." Cally's shoulders tensed. She clutched the notebook tightly to her chest, closing her eyes. "He figured out a niche. Life was hard, and people wore out faster. Kids had accidents working, many of them doing hard things they shouldn't because they had to. A family's survival depended on them. There were no doctors for miles. More folks got sick without treatment or medicine, and many babies died due to poor nutrition and neglect.

"Lonnie started dressing better and kept an ear close to the ground, waiting for news of someone's passing. He'd show up at the house with a pair of black horses and a properly covered cart soon after. He'd respectfully remove his hat and mutter some practiced condolences. Then he'd suggest that he'd be willing to give the deceased a respectful sendoff if the family was short on funds, and almost everyone was. Lonnie became a self-designated undertaker of sorts."

The adrenaline rush is fading away, and Jamie is suddenly very tired. Her twisted ankle is swollen and throbbing hard, but she listens intently as Cally continues talking in a monotone voice. She knows what Cally says might be their only way out of the cellar.

"Lonnie assured them there was no need to waste money they didn't have on a fancy service, resulting in another debt they couldn't pay. For a few dollars, he'd take the body away with him right on the spot, saving them the trouble of disposal or a funeral. The suffering families believed in his good intentions, always grateful for his considerate offer. He'd make haste in bringing those ripe bodies back here to this house, down to this cellar, refusing to touch them any further. My grandmother handled and inspected the bodies, ensuring nothing of value remained before he disposed of them. She pulled out scraps of gold in their teeth, removed buttons from clothing to be reused or sold, and did all manner of ghoulish work, making sure Lonnie would be satisfied. If someone arrived in a casket the family already owned, he used a sharp blade, cutting the shiny satin fabric away cleanly, then broke up the varnished wood to burn in the fireplace. Elizabeth sewed tiny dresses from the tainted fabric. Lonnie checked her work, making sure her painstaking stitches were small enough, then sold the dresses to his friends' wives, claiming they recently arrived from Paris along with dresses he claimed he bought for Elizabeth. She locked herself in a room, pulling a quilt tightly over herself when he took the bodies away after she finished with them. The sounds coming up from this cellar were unimaginable."

Jamie shivered violently, wrapping her arms around her knees tight, trying to control her horror.

"Here? He brought them down here?" Jamie looked frantically around the cellar, hoping nothing of the story remained in her line of sight. Cally sounded weaker.

"Instead of treating the newly dead with respect, providing the burial he assured folks would take place, Lonnie hitched up the horses and pulled the heavy stone cover off the old dry well over there." Cally jerked her head to the left, and the open wound on the back gushed red. "He heaved all those bodies down the well, careful to keep it covered, hiding the stench while they rotted."

Jamie fought back a gag.

"He grew wealthy as the bodies piled higher and bought farm foreclosures for pennies on the dollar calling the land, Crees Crossing. Lonnie firmly established himself as a respectable business owner, but my grandmother knew the truth."

Cally was crying again, her face almost unrecognizable under the mask of blood and filth. Jamie moved in closer, careful not to touch her.

"Elizabeth was shown the light by a group of old women who secretly cared for her after her mother died. They lived together in a shack deep in the woods, watching out for the neglected young girl, keeping her from harm and illness, hiding baskets of bread and fruit for her to find when her father left her alone and hungry. They raised fat wild sheep and tended tangled gardens of herbs. The women needed nothing from anyone to survive. They protected Elizabeth, making sure she didn't fall into the darkness always lurking close by. They were her moral compass, and their ancient teachings were her only playmates. My grandmother watched thoughtfully, learning from this gathering of women. She knew she would be damned for eternity if she didn't do right by the dead, pale bodies dumped without ceremony onto a hard table. She secretly washed them with respect and whispered words taught by the women over their corpses. Threading a needle with waxed black thread, she lovingly took a stitch up through the nose and down through the mouth in each one, making sure they were at rest. She placed sweet herbs she grew in a secret garden into their mouths for a final taste of life before he threw them down the well to decay. Elizabeth kept an accounting of sorts, assigning a number to each soul, intending to keep their memory somehow."

Jamie hung on her words but damn.

"All of these awful things happened?" Jamie whispered. The dreadful thought paralyzed her with fear; there was so much to understand.

"Yes, I told you, these things all happened right here." Cally continued with her explanation, dangerously calm now. "One day, Lonnie caught my grandmother applying her skills and was furious she defied him in any way. He didn't allow her to worship any god or demon. He beat Elizabeth with his fists and leather strap again, and she wanted to take the place of the body on the table. Trying to save herself, out of her mind with pain, she cried out, threatening to tell what he had done for so many years. In a black rage, Lonnie tied her up and locked her in this cellar for days without food or water after he cut out her tongue. Yeah, he cut out her tongue so she couldn't scream, and that's why she never spoke again."

Jamie was shocked. Miz Elizabeth would know peace if it was the last thing she ever did.

"How do you know this is true?" Jamie wondered if the bloody-faced girl was lying. The story was so dreadful. Cally rolled her eyes at Jamie, spitting out a massive clot of blood.

"I heard all this shit growing up like it was some kind of ridiculous family urban legend. I never really listened or cared. Family drama doesn't concern me as long as I get money and whatever I want. They say when Lonnie finally pulled her up from here, she was a ghost. Her skin was transparent, and any clothing she put on tore through it, so she only wore thin white cotton nightgowns ever again. Lonnie died a few months after he did that to her. They found him over there on those steps with a broken back."

There was a loud banging on the floor above, then a lot of yelling, or maybe singing. The two young women instinctively moved closer to each other, both of them staring at the ceiling. Cally lowered her voice.

"No one saw Lonnie posturing around town for a while. I guess someone came to the house looking for him and found him stiff and cold as if he slipped and fell. My grandmother didn't let anyone know the man was missing because she didn't want him to come back. No one knows exactly what happened to him, but my father believes she cursed the asshole and caused him to die painfully and broken because he robbed the dead of their dignity. I think she had other plans for him for what he did to her."

"Did you know Miz Elizabeth, your grandmother, at all? She was such a sweetheart." Jamie wants her black and white notebook of recipes back in her possession. Cally doesn't get to rob her of the lovely moments she shared with her.

"I didn't see her much growing up. She lived in this house alone. I'd spend time with my shitty excuse for a father every once in a while. Mostly the maids took care of me. He'd stop by her house, usually only when he needed money for his whores or gambling, and he used me to get her to let him in. She was okay to me. It wasn't like she was a normal grandparent or anything. She was scary, like a ghost with bare feet and long hair, all dressed in white. She never spoke. Her fingers were ink-stained from writing all the time. I remember her patting me on the head and giving me a piece of candy. I didn't see her when I got older, and I don't know much more. I think she got sick with pneumonia. My dickwad father brought her to the hospital and left her there. He wanted to get ahold of all the land she still owned, planning to sell it and move away, leaving me stuck here alone. The rat bastard started filing legal papers, intending to declare her incompetent, but it takes time. A judge needs to sign off on them. She stayed at Mercy until today, so you say."

"Is that why you came to work there? So, you could be with her and get to know her better?" Jamie hoped hard for even a little something to still like about Cally. She's a miserable excuse for anything good.

"No, you dumb Bitch, I started working at that shit hole trying to find out where she hid all the money, you idiot! She had PILES of it, and her gnarly old ass sure didn't need it anymore! My half-brother TJ, he's the fat-fucking moron upstairs, is in some trouble with a bunch of M&M's. Oh yeah, that's right, you're not so intelligent after all, little miss New Girl. A bunch of badass moonshiners and meth heads over in the next county. Those freaks riled him up, telling him they hear stories about some kind of safe buried in this house. The batshit old cow probably kept the combo in her room with her at Mercy, and I wanted to nose around, you know, act like I give a shit, but noooooo. . . she was YOUR patient and off-limits. I didn't have enough time to try and find out any details before she croaked. TJ and I plan on a 50/50 split. It's my ticket out of here, and he gets to stay alive a while longer if he doesn't fuck it up. I guess he made a deal with that bearded creep and his big old knife. He doesn't have enough sense to do much alone. I didn't give a flying fuck about her. Why the hell would I?"

These are the saddest words Jamie has ever heard, and her tears now are for Miz Elizabeth and all she managed to survive.

The cellar doors crash open, and Jamie and Cally both scurry to a dark corner. TJ waddles down the narrow steps covered in so much blood, grease, and God only knows what else. His eyes look demented, and he's gnawing the meat off a large bone.

"How you girls holding up?" His words slur as he stumbles to the corner.

He whacks Cally on the side of her head with the bone, opening her wound. The revolting person mushes his hand hard in the gash, sucks it off his thumb, then smears the rest across his cheeks like clown makeup. Cally lunges clumsily at him, her sticky hand grabbing at his leg, trying to pull him down. She misses entirely and hits the floor.

"TJ, you stinky pile of dog shit! You won't find anything, ever, if you don't let me out of here. You can't wipe your ass without me!"

Jamie watched them silently. Her training tells her Cally has a severe concussion or possibly something worse. Her movements are choppy, and she's struggling to stay upright.

"We said we'd split the money once I found the combination to the safe or wherever the old hag keeps it buried. I haven't found it yet, but it has to be here somewhere." She's pawing at the air, not able to see clearly. TJ laughs at her, swatting her hands away like flies.

"You took too damn long, and Bart says we need the cash now. He's sick of waiting and wants to get out of town. We decided to snatch you so you wouldn't rat us out, but the other bitches got in the way of our idea. You caused more work for us, and now Bart says you'll be the one to pay. Hope you enjoyed your girl time," TJ sneers at them. "But the fun's just gettin' started, ladies! Soon as Bad Bart upstairs is done with the cookin' in a couple of hours or so, and I don't mean he's making a pie if you get my drift, we've got some exciting party games planned I think you'll like! Well, maybe not, but anyway, we'll be playin' them all the same, and I bet it won't be you girls who win!" TJ winks grotesquely at Jamie, licking his lips. He's holding out the bone on the front of his overalls in an obscene gesture.

"Don't be acting as if you've ever even done it. You're a walking pigsty. No female still alive will ever want your gross lard ass. That old bone is the only action you'll ever get." Cally isn't finished with him yet. She's still looking for a fight. "We agreed to split the money.

You said yes to the deal. Now you change the fucking rules thinking I'll tell you anything?"

His buggy eyes drift to the other side of the cellar, where Lila's body grows colder. He stumbles over to it and pokes at her with the bone. He reaches inside of what's left of the top she has on.

"You know, we might even play with this pretty one some more too. You know people like to say nothin' good happens after midnight, but I think it just might happen tonight." TJ is roaming around the room, whistling at the females, living and dead, laughing at his own joke. He's still rubbing himself with the bone. His high-pitched giggling makes Jamie's stomach turn hard, and she vomits at his feet. TJ kicks at her as he works his way back towards the stairs, but Cally isn't giving up yet.

"I got the combo, you dip shit, I got it right HERE!" She lunges at her half-brother, pointing at some numbers written on a page, waving the creased notebook at him. TJ can't see anything in the dingy light of the cellar, so he shifts his substantial weight and punches Cally solidly in the jaw. She tumbles to the floor, out cold.

"You're full of shit, bitch. You really do think I'm stupid. Stick your schoolwork up your ass where you might learn something." T. J. is rubbing his fingers. They sting from his punch.

Jamie grabs for her friend, sliding the notebook between their bodies as he moves toward the stairs. Cally's blood covers most of the corner now, so she repositions herself even further away from TJ, watching it spread. She knows Cally is fading fast. There's too much on the floor.

"You come at me again, bitch, and I'll make damn sure Bart gets fired up BIG time! My friend Bart, I guess you can call him a friend if you play it straight. He isn't so right in the head. I think maybe his Mama messed him up bad or maybe it was the hard time he did. The boy's handsome in his way, and the other prisoners liked him a lot. He tells me all about it when we're nice and high, lots of details. I'm not real sure but anyway, let me tell you a little story."

Jamie looks around again for something to knock him out, but the cellar offers no solution. She can't handle much more of him.

"A couple of months ago, two ol' gals working for him get brave, dipping into his product when they should be focusing on sellin' it over in Tilbert County, where the market is solid. Bart only plays games when he feels up to it, and he quits playing fast when he figures out their little game of stealin' from him. So, we bring them out here, and he chats them up, saying how beautiful they are and all. We've got beer and pretzels, music turned up loud, real romantic stuff. He gets 'em good and high with as much of his best rock as they can handle. The girls are all sweet and lovey-dovey. I swear they have those stars in their eyes you read about in books. Bart strips them naked and gets them nice and juicy, and he makes them dance for us. Woo-wee, I about peed myself. Those nasty girls were rubbing and kissing all over us and each other too. You ever see that? I'm guessing you might before we finish our business here, not that I want to see Cally's big ol' ass again anytime soon. But hey, who knows, the night's young. When Bart got bored with the fun, he tied them up. Man, they were ready for some action, and I had my share of the playtime too. Take that, Cally, you dog-stinkin' whore, are you listening? I have done it with a real live chick.

"Then Bart cranked up his chainsaw and took it to the plain one, making sure the other watched close. I helped, but it was messy with all the noise and screaming and stuff flying around, so I got us burgers while he finished up. But THEN the other one? Well, she was good-looking in a used-up way, and he liked her a little better, so when he finished up doin' her, and I mean he did everything and then some, he knocked her ass out and took her out to the old field way in the back. It was a hot day out there. He smeared handfuls of honey all over and up in her, making sure she was covered up good, working it into all the holes and cracks. Then he tied her on top of a humungous fuckin' fire ant hill—and this is so funny, you're gonna' love this—he cut her tongue out so she couldn't even scream! MY idea, I remembered hearing about grandma, pretty damn clever, right? After all, it's a family tradition. We came back to look at her after a week or so. She'd been picked clean down to the bone in most places. It was so cool. Those crazy-ass fire ants ate off almost all her skin. Not much left for the pack of dogs who finally came sniffing around. Chew on THAT thought awhile. What a way to go. I'm tellin' you Bart knows how to get it done in style. So, if you bitches want the much quicker friends and family treatment, you'd best knock off your shit while you're still able."

TJ howls with laughter, clamoring up the steps and banging the doors shut again.

She's hurting terribly and can't put weight on her ankle to stand, and it's swollen up twice its usual size. Most likely sprained or fractured. She needs to find a way out before they come back down, or she'll die horribly in this hideous place. Jamie's thinking hard, desperate to make a move, and the notebook lies open next to her on the floor where Cally is still in a heap, barely breathing. She glances at the notebook, feeling completely hopeless, wishing she'd lose her mind completely. It's all so dark and awful. In the shifting shadows of the cellar, she sees the words and numbers written on the pages as clearly as if someone is holding a flashlight. They are moving slightly, forming sentences right before her eyes.

"Seven to heaven, ring the bell to hell. Add clover and meadowfoam to hide the smell. Drip the candle, and the wax will seal. Remember the salt so the body can heal."

Jamie reads the words out loud, feeling the musty air in the cellar grow colder.

"What in the?" She picks up the black and white pasteboard notebook, holding it closer to her face. The words of the *recipe* are crystal clear now.

"Wash the flesh and wipe away the blood. Swallow a tear for the night's new love. Needle the heart and tie the thread. No rest for you yet. There's work for the dead."

Jamie can't breathe as the awful smell becomes worse. She hears something tapping, clicking lightly on the floor.

Oh shit, NO, not the rats, PLEASE!!!

Lila's right hand is moving. Her fingers are moving up and down, making sounds on the floor with her blood-caked fingernails.

But she's DEAD! SHE'S FUCKING DEAD!

Jamie's brain screams in her head as Lila slowly starts to rise off the floor into a crossed-legged sitting position. Her head lolls to one side, and her eyelids flutter as she tries gathering and arranging the snarled mess of remaining hair into a bun like she usually wears it. Jamie is in shock. She can't move. Lila gazes at her lovingly, twitching the corners of her mouth as if to smile, right before Jamie finally gives in, and everything in the cellar turns black.

Someone is humming as she tries to remember where she is, blinking rapidly, struggling to return to the world as it is on this harrowing night. With a faintly stamped flower design still visible on the thin fabric, the worn flour sack is over Cally's head now. The fraying twine handles are knotted tightly around her neck, and Jamie makes out the letters "E.C." stitched in black through the blood.

Her chest heaves with enormous effort in a single breath. Jamie understands Cally is dead.

Her beautiful friend Lila or whatever she is now is sitting on the steps, humming something random to herself. Holding a finger to her lips, she whispers.

"Shhhhhhh."

Jamie doesn't know or care at this minute if she is still alive or also dead. These things can't be happening. It's not possible. She drags herself over against the farthest wall, grateful now for the chewing sounds of the creatures living within. At least they are real. She waits as the pain in her body and dreadful thoughts in her mind give her a renewed kind of sanity; or she'll gladly welcome insanity if it means this will end soon. She watches her friend and can't help feeling sad for Lila, who's still wearing only the scraps of her tattered clothing. She looks so alone.

Lila sits quietly, nibbling on her blackened tongue, patting her hair as it snakes down the torn skin of her face. She's looking at the shattered bones poking up through her skin, curiously examining her fatal wounds as if she's her own nursing patient. She digs a finger deep into the ragged edges of Bart's viscous knife slashes to her leg. Jamie tries standing again, but the pain in her ankle forces her back down. She's not afraid of Lila, no matter what she is, and considers hugging her broken and battered doll of a lost friend, wanting to comfort her.

The sounds coming from upstairs suddenly stop. Jamie hears the voices of two men talking not far away, then what sounds like a truck engine sputter and start-up, grinding and spitting. After a few loud pops, the noise stops.

No, Ma'am, it's a chainsaw, her brain tells her. The thing resembling Lila jumps off the stairs.

"Shhhhhhh."

With a bent finger pressed to her lips, she silences Jamie again, moving at an inhuman speed behind one of the wooden barrels as the cellar doors open. Jamie notices the sky above isn't as dark now; it's closer to daylight. She holds her breath as the two men lurch forward down the steps, holding each other upright, slopping beer on themselves.

"Wakey, wakey, bitches, almost time for eggs, and YOUR ASSES ON A PLATTER!" Bart is in the center of the room laughing and singing as he waves the rusty chainsaw around while TJ, who's wearing only a pair of stained boxer shorts, performs a perverted dance, humping against Bart. His soft belly flops as they circle the room like trained animals in a circus act.

"Well, now, what do we have here?" Bart pulls the sack off Cally's head. "Did you do this all by yourself, little lady? I say it's self-defense, Your Honor. This dead-ass-bitch is messed up. I bet she put up a hell of a fight trying to get to you first. I love a good catfight. Damn, I'm impressed." He squints at Jamie, grinning maliciously.

He's drunk and high, jabbing the chainsaw at Cally's neck. He's obsessed with the notion Jamie killed her and claps loudly, still holding the saw in one hand, bowing in Jamie's direction.

"My hat's off to you, girly. Should I warm this baby up? We'll get rid of her properly, and I promise you can help." He's fumbling with the pull-start on the side, unable to coordinate the movement of his hands to re-start the chainsaw. He drops the well-used tool, and sparks fly as the metal hits the concrete floor then bounces away. "Damn, guess I need to get me a new one for the next party." Bart sits down on the floor near Jamie, about to pass out, unable to keep his eyes open, and his head snaps up, making his dark beard jiggle every time he opens them.

TJ is slugging down a beer with one hand while peeing on Cally's body, holding his small penis in the other.

"Always wanted to piss on her. I think she kind of likes it." He crumples the empty beer can, flinging it hard at her face, leaving a new opening in her skin, then staggers over to the dusty glass mason jars on the shelves, trying to pry one open with his teeth. Jamie hopes he succeeds, and the spoiled contents are appealing enough to poison him on the spot.

She's ready to fight until her last breath. They won't be impaired forever, and she needs to make her getaway. Lila still crouches in silence behind the barrel. Jamie can barely make out the shape of her friend but sees the stark white bone gleaming through the skin of her arm. Lila moves uncertainly, balancing on her splayed, broken toes to a standing position. Jamie's jaw drops open. She shoves her fist in her mouth, stifling a scream, as the once beautiful abomination rises off the floor. She spirals ungracefully to the ceiling, moaning softly. TJ drops the mason jar he's trying to open. It shatters, spilling the awful contents.

"What the fuck are you doing?" he says to Jamie, bending down, almost toppling over his drooping gut. The sloppy man picks up a large piece of the broken glass, slashing his hand. "Fuck me. Now, I'm going to cut your throat, bitch. I'm hungry, and you're no fun. Bart's out of it, so I'm in charge of this party now." TJ lunges at Jamie, but his short, flabby arms can't reach far enough, and he loses his footing.

Lila is above them now, hovering like a horrible human parade balloon in the stagnant air, carefully considering the scene below. She jerks like a mechanical toy, unhinging joint by joint, as she spreads her arms out wide. When she drops, Jamie covers her eyes with the notebook, aware it provides absolutely no protection, but instinctively trying to save herself anyway.

The stink in the room amplifies to a dense fog of putrid moisture as TJ's blood sprays over her. Jamie screams over and over, as hard as she can, trying to drown out the sounds of bones crunching and flesh tearing. TJ's shrieking no longer sounds like anything remotely human, and even when it stops, Jamie knows the madness isn't over. Lila bites off dripping mouthfuls of flesh, chewing loudly, as her teeth saw through Bart's neck. The big man thrashes like a rabid animal, trying to throw her off to no avail. When she's finished, Lila wipes her mouth on her useless arm, casually tossing his decapitated head on top of the steaming heap of gore, TJ's remains. Jamie faints again. Her mind is no longer able to function.

The black and white composition notebook still curled up in Jamie's hand feels cool and refreshing against her feverish cheek. She appreciates the soothing feeling of the cardboard. Opening one eye, she's shocked at what looks like weeping grey matter sticking to it.

Oh PLEASE, no more, PLEASE, I can't.

Lila is sitting in the middle of the unspeakable mess. Her fingers fumble like butterflies with crushed wings, still trying to shape her hair into a proper bun. Jamie is sobbing so hard she can barely see but cannot look away from Lila, who holds her hands together on the side of what used to be her beautiful face like a child who needs a nap. Jamie hears the rats in the walls make a sound like a word: *rest.* She opens the offal-smeared notebook. She's panting as her trembling fingers turn to the final page. Written under the ingredients for *"Wild Mushroom Stew"* is a series of numbers listed repeatedly in faded black ink, and then the words, *"Grant them peace and give sleep. Kiss the cheek and no more weep."* She understands her friend Lila returned to help save her life, and it no longer matters how because Jamie can't comprehend any of it right now. She uses what little remains of her strength and willpower to slowly drag herself through the human carnage over to Lila, who sits rocking and humming mindlessly. It takes more courage than the devastated young woman has or believes is possible to touch her friend's hand gently. Lila's eyes are lifeless and hollow, but she tilts her head, gazing at the wall in Jamie's direction. Jamie props herself up high enough to gently kiss what remains intact of her precious friend's cheek.

"Thank you," Jamie breathes gently into her ear. Lila's eyes flutter several times, and her ruined lips form what may be a smile. Then she fades away in a thin plume, to nothing. Jamie weeps huge gulping sobs for the loss of her friend.

She must get herself out of the stomach-churning stench of death and piles of human remains in the cellar before her wounds are infected. Jamie uses the blood-soaked floor to help her slide over to the notebook one last time. The pain is excruciating as she shoves the damp pages into the waistband of her pants. The steep steps are the only way out of the cellar. She doesn't care how long it takes to maneuver herself up them, time is meaningless, but it feels like an eternity. Her entire body is throbbing, and her wounds burn like red hot pokers with each movement. The monsters didn't slam the heavy wooden doors shut behind them. They are open wide. Jamie takes a deep breath, wincing as her cracked ribs shift in her chest, and she screams to the sky above, painted with the colors of sunrise. One more step. The sun is coming up over the gnarled trees surrounding this house of sorrow. The first of the falling leaves do a slow ballet, twirling in the fresh morning air. She will be free with the next pull of her arms. Jamie sighs, looking back one last time. She's sorry to be escaping by herself. But she's comforted knowing Lila will take good care of her special patient, Miz Elizabeth, forever.

The End

RUTHANN JAGGE

Ruthann grew up in Upstate New York, where her favorite month of October is magical.

She writes dark speculative fiction and horror.

Numerous successful anthologies feature her work, with solo projects planned for release in 2022.

Extensive travel, superstition, and backyard boogeymen influence her characters and settings.

She lives on a cattle ranch in Texas with her husband and his animals.

A large, blended family keeps her sane most of the time.

Member HWA.

www.ruthannjagge.com

ABOUT THE EDITOR / PUBLISHER

Dawn Shea is an author and half of the publishing team over at D&T Publishing. She lives with her family in Mississippi. Always an avid horror lover, she has moved forward with her dreams of writing and publishing those things she loves so much.

D&T Previously published material:
    ABC's of Terror
    After the Kool-Aid is Gone

Follow her author page on Amazon for all publications she is featured in.
    Follow D&T Publishing at the following locations:
    Website
    Facebook: Page / Group
    Or email us here: dandtpublishing20@gmail.com

Produced by D&T Publishing LLC

The New Girls' Patient by Ruthann Jagge

Edited by Patrick C. Harrison III

Cover by Don Noble

Formatting by J.Z. Foster

Corinth, MS

Made in the USA
Las Vegas, NV
27 November 2022

60464530R00025